SOME LIKE IT HOT: WRITING SEX AND ROMANCE

Crafting Unputdownable Fiction

BETH YARNALL

SOME LIKE IT HOT: WRITING SEX AND ROMANCE

COPYRIGHT

Copyright © 2017 by Beth Yarnall

All rights reserved.

No part of this book may be reproduced in any form or by any electronic or mechanical means, including information storage and retrieval systems, without written permission from the author, except for the use of brief quotations in a book review.

Cover by: Go On Write

ebook ISBN: 9781940811710

print ISBN: 9781940811604

SOME LIKE IT HOT: WRITING SEX AND ROMANCE

INTRODUCTION

Romance novels have gotten a bad rap over the years—mommy porn, bodice rippers, frustrated housewives. I have a theory on why that is. Romance is written for, by, and about women. It's the ultimate feminist manifesto. That intimidates some people. They think that romance novels set unrealistic expectations for women. Nonsense. Romance shows women that they can have loving, supportive, and fulfilling relationships. That they *deserve* all of those things.

And *orgasms*.

And why not? Don't you want your children to hold out for someone who loves, respects, and appreciates them? Don't you want that for yourself? Romance novels not only make us believe it's possible to have healthy, vital relationships, they help us demand such relationships. Romance novels are subversive. They're uplifting. Romance itself is an ultimate life experience.

Look at movies and TV. You'll often find romance even in the most hard-core stories. *Terminator* and *Star Wars* have romance plots. Strong romance plots drove TV shows like *Castle*, *Moonlighting*, and *Cheers*. It was the sexual tension that made us tune in each week to find out if this would be the episode where they finally acted on their attraction. Twitter blew up when Sheldon and Amy finally kissed on *The Big Bang Theory*, then blew up all over again when they consummated their relationship.

In this book I'm going to show you how to plot a romance like you'd plot any other element of your novel. You'll learn about sexual tension, the stages of intimacy, levels of heat from sweet to erotic, and how to write sex scenes that don't read like a how-to manual.

Ready to get sexy?

AUTHOR'S NOTE

In this book I've presented samples from other authors' work (with proper credit) as well as my own. Not because I think my writing is special or precious, but because sometimes it was the most expedient way for me to illustrate a particular point. I could talk all day long about how to do something, but sometimes that's not enough. You have to see the principle in action in order to fully take it in.

I hope you enjoy these authors' excerpts as much as I do and will consider reading one or more of their books. Many are award-winning and best-selling authors. I promise you won't be disappointed.

1. PLOTTING A ROMANCE

To make the distinction between characters easier I'm going to use hero/male and heroine/female. However, everything I talk about applies equally to same-sex couples and multiple partners.

Whether you're a plotter or a pantser (write by the seat of your pants) there are some romance 'have to's' to keep in mind while plotting and writing your novel. I consider myself a pantser who learned how to plot...sort of. I find I write faster when I at least have an outline with plot points or tent poles that prop the story up throughout the book, thus avoiding the sagging middle. Then I pants my way from tent pole to tent pole. Every writer is different. There is no right way to write a book. *There is only your way*.

In mystery novels there will always be a mystery

to solve (most likely murder), clues along the way, a red herring or two, and the perpetrator will get caught in the end. Those are the genre promises—a formula readers understand and count on. Can you imagine reading an entire mystery novel only to find out that the bad guy gets away? That's like a thriller with no ticking time clock or world to save. Or a sci-fi book with no futuristic scientific elements, advanced technology or extraterrestrial life.

We call that kind of book a *wall banger* because the author didn't fulfill the genre promise, making you want to throw the book at the wall. Nothing will make a reader more frustrated than an author not following through on the genre promise. As with any genre, there are inherent reader promises or—'have to's'—in romance.

The Rules of Romance

1. The hero and heroine should meet in the first three chapters. Ideally, they should meet in the first chapter, but definitely by the third. Really though, get them together on the page as soon as possible!
2. The 'meet cute' is a must. It's when the hero and heroine meet for the first time.

It can be as funny as the hero coming across a woman walking down the side of the road in a beaver suit (Susan Elizabeth Phillips's *Natural Born Charmer*) or suspenseful, like the hero discovering that the heroine is the reporter who burned him as a spy and got his best friend killed (***Far From Honest*** by Beth Yarnall—coming soon). The only thing that matters is that it's memorable!

3. The use of tropes. At least two or three per book. Some examples are: friends to lovers, marriage/engagement of convenience, secret baby, reunited lovers, forbidden romance, and so on. We'll go into these in more depth later.

4) There must be something keeping the lovers apart. *Real* conflict. A real reason why it would *never* work out between the two of them. It can't be something that's easily solved with a conversation, or what I call *Three's Company* conflict (I'm dating myself). Usually the conflict stems from their backstory and their goals and motivation. Debra Dixon wrote a great book called *GMC: Goal, Motivation, and Conflict* that's become *the* bible for writing

books with strong conflict arising from characters' goals and motivation. Read it!

5) There must be something keeping them physically together/forced proximity. This could be a trope such as a snowed-in cabin or a pretend marriage. It could also be circumstantial, like being in/planning their friend's wedding (especially a destination wedding) or the two of them working on a project that will make or break their career/business. If the couple isn't together for the majority of the story then it's going to be really difficult for them to fall in love.

6) The book *has to* end in a happily ever after or a happy for now. The couple *must* be together in some way at the end of the book, either with a marriage, a promise of marriage, or a real sense that the couple is headed toward forever. This is the hallmark of romance. It's the genre promise to the reader. If either the hero or heroine is dead by the end of the book it's not a romance (unless they're both ghosts). Shakespeare's *Romeo and Juliet*, the movie *Ghost* with Patrick Swayze and Demi Moore, and most of Nicolas Sparks's books are not romances—they're tragedies. Romance readers expect a 'ride off into the sunset' moment for the couple at the end of the book. Don't disappoint them!

Romance Novel Tropes

What are tropes? The dictionary defines a trope as a 'figure of speech'. In novels it's storytelling shorthand for a story concept readers will instantly recognize and understand. As children we were exposed to tropes such as the ugly duckling, the prince disguised as a commoner, a wish that becomes a curse, the evil witch or stepmother, the poor girl who wins the prince, the unexpected hero, and so on. Tropes are used in fiction because they work. I bet you conjured up a story to go along with the children's book tropes I listed above, such as Cinderella, Snow White or Pinocchio. Tropes work exactly the same way in romance. The reader knows what kind of story they're getting before they even open the book.

Romance tropes:

- Accidental pregnancy
- All grown up
- Amnesia
- Arranged marriage
- At odds/working against each other
- Baby of convenience
- Bait & switch—thinks hero/heroine is perfect for someone else then decides they want him/her

- Beauty & the Beast
- Betrayal
- Billionaire
- Blackmail
- Bodyguard
- Celebrity and ordinary girl/guy
- Damsel in distress/knight in shining armor
- Disguised—a woman posing as a man or vice versa
- Enemies to lovers
- Family feud
- Fish out of water
- Forbidden love
- Friend's big brother/little sister
- Friends to lovers
- Friends with benefits
- From different worlds/across the tracks
- From ex to next
- Girl/boy next door/love thy neighbor
- Guardian/ward
- Hate at first sight
- High school sweethearts
- Honey trap/lure
- Impersonation
- Love at first sight
- Love triangle

- Make-over story/ugly duckling
- Marriage of convenience
- Masquerade (one of the characters in disguise/not who they say they are)
- Matchmaker
- May-December romance
- Mistaken identity
- Movie star
- Mysterious past
- Nanny to wife
- New old flame
- Stepsiblings/stepparent
- Office affairs
- One night stand
- On the run/road trip
- Operation make him/her jealous
- Opposites attract
- Outsider who shakes up status quo
- Political scandal
- Pretend marriage/fake engagement
- Rags to riches
- Redemption
- Reformed rake/bad boy
- Reincarnation romance
- Reunited lovers
- Revenge
- Rock star

- Royal romance
- Runaway bride/groom
- Second chances
- Secret baby
- Secret crushes
- Secret marriage
- Stranded/snowbound/desert island
- Sudden parenthood/doorstep baby/inherited baby
- The bet
- The lesson/teaching how to catch a lover
- The one that got away
- Twins (secret twins / impersonation)
- Undercover as lovers
- Unrequited love
- Virgin hero or heroine
- Wounded hero/heroine—physically or emotionally

Chances are you have one or more of these tropes in your book regardless of the genre of your novel. This is not a comprehensive list but it is a good jumping-off point in helping you to decide which tropes to use or which tropes you've used without even knowing it. Tropes are not just used in novels but also in movies and TV shows.

Let's have some fun seeing if we can figure out what tropes were used in some classic movies.

The Wizard of Oz: fish out of water, ugly duckling to beautiful swan, and road trip.

Gone with the Wind: enemies to lovers, marriage of convenience, and reformed rake.

Star Wars: Episode IV—A New Hope: outsider who shakes up status quo, royal romance, and love triangle (till we find out Luke is Leia's brother—ew).

Plotting a romance

Plotting a romance novel is very much like plotting any other book. You'll have turning points and obstacles along the way. The hero and heroine will each have their own goals and motivation, which will almost always result in conflict between the couple. They might be at cross-purposes. For example, one of them may love the small town they were born in while the other can't wait to get out of that same town (***Urge and Rare*** by Beth Yarnall). Or in the case of my reporter and burned spy, the hero wants the name of the heroine's source—the person who burned him. She wants protection while she regroups to figure out why her story went south.

You can use any plotting method to plot a romance—Save the Cat, The Hero's Journey, The

W Plot, The Snowflake Method, Michael Hauge's Story Structure, and so on. Whatever works for *you*. You may not hit all the beats of your preferred plotting method while plotting the romance in your novel, but you should hit most of them. It might look a little something like this:

- **Ordinary World:** We see the hero or heroine's normal world before the couple meets. This is also known as the set up.
- **The Meet Cute:** The hero and heroine meet for the first time. It can be funny, surprising (old lover), angry, etc. Make it memorable!
- **Denial:** The hero and heroine deny their attraction for each other. He/she is all wrong for me. I don't want to be attracted to this person. This relationship will ruin me.
- **Acknowledged Interest:** As the attraction grows, they find it harder and harder to resist each other. Somehow, despite how wrong they are for each other, their lips keep meeting.
- **Conflict Intrudes:** There are *reasons* they can't be together. Big, seemingly impossible reasons stemming from

conflict. This is the tipping point—will they act on their attraction or are there just too many reasons not to? Hint: they act on their attraction.

- **Fun and Games:** They finally do the deed and it was awesome! They're ignoring the reasons why they shouldn't be together and basking in how great the sex is. This is where they get to know each other and start to fall in love...
- **Complications Threaten to Push Them Apart:** The tension of the subplot and the reasons they can't/shouldn't be together start to intrude on their warm, fuzzy glow. Everything isn't so rosy. They're being forced to make a choice: give up, or change their initial goal or mindset to make room for the relationship.
- **Together But Not Really:** They're working together/thrown together to overcome the Big Bad (the outside force that's been threatening them all book long, the promise they made to their bestie to be in the wedding, or the reason they can't just get up and walk out). Things are really getting tense and

they now have to make a choice: am I in or am I out?

- **The Black Moment/Climax:** The romance is dead. The conflict is just too impossible to overcome. They cannot be together. At this point the reader should be really, really worried that they're not going to get a happily ever after or happy for now.
- **Change of Heart/Mind:** The hero and/or the heroine has a conversation with a friend or mentor who helps them see how wrong they've been. Or maybe the hero or heroine finally gets what they've wanted all book long (their goal) only to discover it wasn't what they really wanted or needed. This is a serious change of heart and/or mindset. They have to be able to overcome all the obstacles of the black moment.
- **The Grand Gesture:** One of them goes to the other and admits they were wrong, that the relationship can work out. Lots of talking it out/apologizing. Also kissing. Lots and lots of kissing.

HEA/HFN: The happily ever after/happy for now.

The lovers ride off into the sunset together. Sometimes there's a wedding, sometimes not. The reader closes the book on a happy sigh. You fulfilled the genre promise.

Optional Epilogue: Some authors like to provide an extra experience for their readers, a glimpse of the future for the lovers. This could be the wedding that didn't happen at the end of the book. It could be a years-down-the-road look at how their life together turned out or how they're handling parenthood. It could even contain a plot seed planted for the next book in the series.

When I plot out my romantic suspense novels I plot the romance right along side the suspense elements. It's important to make sure the romance storyline advances at the same pace as the other elements of your story, weaving them both together. I often find that the romance ups the ante in the suspense storyline. As their attraction and affection grow so does their desire to keep each other safe. Romance complicates things. Use those complications to the fullest.

2. THE SEX

Oddly, the question I get asked the most, as a romance author is whether I'm writing about my own sex life. Um, no. I'm writing *fiction,* not an autobiography. It's the people on the page getting busy, not me. In contrast, no one's ever asked me if I've killed anyone in real life like I do in my books. And I've killed lots of people...on paper.

As in any scene you write, you have to fully immerse yourself and your reader in what's happening by using deep point of view. It's not you having sex on the page—it's your characters. Each couple you write will be unique in their approach, desire, and experience. But we'll get more into that a little later.

There are distinct levels of heat in romance—

how much action the reader gets on the page from none to *hello Mary!*

Sweet: No sex *at all*. Sweet romances are sometimes called 'clean romances'. They often have a religious message, but not always. Some readers want all of the falling-in-love hearts and flowers without any of the consummating. Sweet romances cross subgenres and are very popular with readers of all ages and backgrounds.

Fade to Black: Closed door sex. We know they're doing the deed, but it all happens off the page. The couple might head to the bedroom, kissing all the way there, and then the scene closes reopening the next morning with them stretching and yawning and having breakfast together. There might be some light petting, but nothing past over-the-sweater action before the scene ends.

Sexy: A voyeur in the bedroom. The reader gets a blow by blow, so to speak, of *all* the action. There might be some flowery words and vague descriptions, but it's eminently clear what's happening when. The reader is right there with the couple, experiencing every sensation as the characters experience them.

Erotic Romance: No more flowers. Descriptions are more detailed, the language is coarser and bawdier, and there's a broader range of sex acts such as BDSM, fetish, multiple partners, multiple genders, and so on. Anything goes as long as it ends with the partners living happily ever after (HEA) or happy for now (HFN).

Erotica: No promises. All the indecent raciness of erotic romance with one notable difference —there's no promise of a HEA or HFN in erotica. For that reason erotica is not considered romance.

LGBTQ+ romance can range from sweet to erotic, just like heterosexual romance. There has been a misconception that just because the characters are gay, bisexual or transgendered the book will automatically be erotic. Not true. Where a character falls on the Kinsey scale (also called the Heterosexual-Homosexual Rating Scale) has no bearing on how hot the book will be.

To Sex or Not to Sex

Do you *need* sex scenes in a romance novel or a novel with romantic elements? Does writing a couple's intimate moments make you squirm in your seat? Are you worried what your mother, grandmother, coworkers, etc. are going to think when they read your book? I felt the same way when my first book was published. My dad asked to read it. My Mormon mother-in-law asked to read it.

Talk about having to get over my embarrassment quick! You will too. I promise everything will be okay. Chances are if you're married, have had significant others or have children the cat's already out of the bag. Your grandma probably knows you're having sex. If she's your grandma *you know* she had sex.

Still, writing sex scenes may be uncomfortable for some of you. One way to tell is how comfortable you are reading them. That's usually the tip-off. Maybe you'd be better off writing on the sweeter side—either no sex at all or fade to black/close the door sex scenes. And that's okay. You don't have to write hot to write romance. Readers will know if you're not comfortable writing sex. I'd rather you not write those scenes than cheat the reader and yourself. So stop reading right now.

Just kidding. There's lots more great information in this book regardless of your heat preference. I'm going to talk about emotional intimacy, sexual tension/attraction, and the stages of physical intimacy. Sex happens in the brain as well as the body. Even if your characters don't go *there* you'll still have to show their physical attraction to one another.

Sex Scenes Have a Purpose

If you can remove the love scenes from your novel and it doesn't make a difference to the romance story line then you need to take a hard look at those scenes. Sex scenes should move the romance forward. No two sex scenes should be the same. The sex the characters have at the beginning of the book will be much different than the sex they have at the end of the story. Their first time will be about chemistry and finally scratching that itch. As the story moves along and they start to fall in love, the sex scenes will become more and more emotional. By the end of the book the sex will be about two people connecting physically *and* emotionally.

Think about your own romantic relationships and how they've grown and changed over time. The longer a couple is together, the closer they become. It's the same with your characters. Sex scenes are an excellent barometer of where the romance is going, how fast it's moving, and how deep it's becoming.

3. THE TWELVE STAGES OF PHYSICAL INTIMACY

I first learned about the twelve stages of physical intimacy from author Linda Howard, who used to give a very popular talk on the subject based on Desmond Morris's *Intimate Behavior: A Zoologist's Classic Study of Human Intimacy*. It's a physical progression of intimacy from eye contact to the sexual act.

Stage One: Eye to body. This is the first 'summing up' or 'noticing' glance where the hero sees the heroine for the first time or vice versa. It's the beginning of their attraction and a great way for the author to work in a character's physical description.

Stage Two: Eye to eye. This is the first active interaction between the hero and heroine. It's the beginning of sexual tension, the recognition of mutual attraction. The across-the-room eye lock can be a powerful moment between the characters. They may even have a physical reaction to their gazes connecting for the first time.

Stage Three: Voice to voice. What the heroine and hero say to each other for the first time is important, as is how it's said. This interaction may set the tone between them for the rest of the story.

Stage Four: Hand to hand (or arm). This is the first physical interaction between the characters. Look where we are—stage four—a third of the way there. That tells us how powerful touch is. The act of holding hands or a touch on the arm can feel very intimate.

Stage Five: Arm to shoulder. The old yawn and drop an arm around the girl move. Why is this a classic? Because this is serious intimacy. The characters' bodies are aligned. It's an act of bringing the other person into your personal space or over to your side.

Stage Six: Arm to waist or back. The hand on the small of the back to guide a woman through the room, or an arm around the waist, is a sign of possession or a she's-with-me signal to the other men in the room. It's an outward sign that these two people are intimate even if they have never had sex.

Stage Seven: Mouth to mouth. The first time the couple acts on the sexual tension arcing between them. The first kiss is an important milestone in a potential relationship. It's intimate. In movies there's a big swell of music as their lips meet. This is what all of that eye contact and tentative touching was leading to.

Stage Eight: Hand to head. Sometimes happens during the first kiss. Hand to face is a very intimate touch. The brush of a thumb across a cheek and down the neck, hands in hair are both *very* intimate.

A quick aside here: I worked for several years as a hairstylist and makeup artist. In the salon we used to joke that the cutting cape was like Wonder Woman's lasso. Clients would spill *very* personal details of their lives—secrets even their therapist or significant other might not know. That's how intimate the hand-to-head touch is. If you think about it, four out of five of our senses are in our head. Not only that, but our ability to breath (nose and mouth) and our fragile throat are exposed in this stage. Allowing someone to touch your face and head is an act of trust.

Stage Nine: Hand to body. The beginning of

foreplay. We haven't reached the point of no return yet. It's a key place to have your characters doubt if this is really what they want. They might pull back a little before deciding to commit.

Stage Ten: Mouth to breast. We're fully into foreplay now. This might be a great close-but-no-cigar moment for your couple. They get really wound up, only to have some outside force or internal conflict prevent them from 'going all the way'. A cooling off, if you will.

Stage Eleven: Hand to genitals. We're pretty much at the point of no return, but there is some major mileage to be gained from messing with your characters in these final stages. There's also nothing saying that your characters can't hang out at this stage for a while. There's a lot of pleasure to be found on the road to bending the bedposts.

Stage Twelve: Genitals to genitals. Touchdown! This is the moment the characters have been fighting against/dying for. It's the point of no return. Sex complicates things. It changes *everything* between your characters.

You don't have to check each stage off like a checklist as you write your book. I just wanted you to be aware of how intimate your characters are getting and give you ideas on how to show the progression of the relationship. It's okay to skip a stage, or linger and explore a particular stage. You don't have to take your characters all the way to stage twelve either. Have fun with your characters. Tie them up in knots. Make them ache for each other.

Note: In romance, consent is ***everything***. No means no. You can ruin the rapport your reader has with your hero or heroine by breaking this rule. Rape isn't sexy. It certainly isn't romantic.

4. SEXUAL TENSION

The reader has to believe the hero and heroine as a couple. When we initially meet a potential mate our first reaction is physical. Have you ever broken it off with someone because there was just no chemistry between the two of you? Chemistry and sexual tension in a romance is vital. It's what keeps the reader turning the page to find out *will they or won't they?* Use the twelve stages of intimacy to help you create sexual tension between your characters. Build it slowly over time—a touch here, a lingering look there.

Here's an excerpt from **Liberate** by Beth Yarnall in which the hero sees the heroine for the first time:

I follow Cora into the reception area. Savannah blocks whoever it is she's talking to so I can't see who it is, but whoever they are, they're small, much smaller than Savannah's five-nine frame. Savannah shifts, revealing a pastel confection of a young woman about Cora's age.

All lace and silk, she's sweet-looking in her soft colors like she just walked out of a Sunday church service. But the look in her eyes is wary... suspicious...jaded, reminding me of angry, hard prison stares. This chick's seen some shit. More than that, she's experienced some shit, has maybe even done some shit. She's a survivor. This I understand. I recognize her in the same way I recognize the new man that stares back at me in the mirror.

Her costume is nearly perfect. I bet if I sniffed her she'd smell like baby powder and lemons. I edge closer to her. She catches me with a sudden flick of a glance, freezing me where I stand. Everything about her shouts *Back the fuck off.* It only makes me want to draw closer. Who is she? Who or what made her this way? And why does she look at me like she knows who I am? Not the TV-news-segment me, but the real me, the Beau deep down inside.

For the first time since I got out of prison I don't feel alone. There really are others out there like me. One of them is standing mere feet in front of me, regarding me with the same guarded, expectant look I'm wearing.

And she's *beautiful*.

Not the usual tinglies most people get when they see someone for the first time and are attracted to them. Beau recognizes himself—or at least aspects of himself—in the heroine. He also acknowledges her beauty, but that's not what intrigues him about her. Beau just got out of prison. In this scene I tried to use his backstory to draw him toward the heroine.

There has to be something *more* between the hero and heroine than just their attractiveness. They have to be intrigued, drawn in by more than looks. When creating your characters try to consider not only who would be a perfect match for them but also who would be the absolute *worst* person they could fall in love with. Take the spy and reporter in my earlier example. She burned the hero and got his best friend killed when she broke her story on TV. For him, falling in love with her would be a disaster, right? But it sure does make it fun.

When writing intimate scenes you want the reader to *feel* how crazy your characters are for each other. Keep them on the edge of their seat by building the sexual tension slowly and methodically from the first moment they meet, so that when the characters finally do get at it the reader is like "YES, *finally*." The reader should be as invested in the relationship as the characters are.

Here's an excerpt from the **Innocent serial** by Beth Yarnall:

I run my fingers around the edge of his face. I feel like I'm just now seeing him. We keep touching each other, little discovering touches. He leans in and smells me, nuzzling his nose along my jawline to my ear. My hands are in his hair, sifting through strands that are softer than I thought they'd be. I breathe him in like he did me and he makes a noise at the back of his throat that tests the limits I just set for myself.

"Cora." He sounds agonized.

I know how he feels. I ache in places I didn't know could be so electric and sensitive and *alive*. All of my senses are on alert for what he'll say or do next.

"We have to stop."

I'm confused. *Why?*

"God, not here." He catches my face in his hands, stopping me from licking the spot just below his ear. He gives me a quick kiss. "If you keep that up we're going to give the neighbors a show and what I have planned for you is very, very private."

"You have plans for me?"

Putting his forehead to mine, he makes a frustrated noise. "You have no idea."

This cheers me immensely.

This is a pretty chaste scene yet it's full of sexual tension. These two are *very* attracted to each other. The scenting of each other, inhaling the pheromones they're putting off, and the small touches of the face and hair spark their desire for each other. Note the internal thoughts of the heroine and the words of the hero. Their clothes are on, but it's still a pretty hot scene. There's no doubt these two have chemistry.

Most of the books I write are pretty spicy, so I wanted to give you an example of sexual tension from a sweet romance.

Here's an excerpt from **Home to Montana** by Charlotte Carter:

Without even looking up, she knew the moment Nick entered her row of pews. She tensed. Goose flesh rose on her arms as he sat next to her. Not too close, but close enough that she was aware of the breadth of his shoulders, the firmness of his thighs stretching the dark blue denim of his jeans, the way he linked his strong fingers together between his knees and bowed his head.

Oh, dear... How was she supposed to concentrate on the church service with Nick sitting next to her? Or find the peace she usually did in church?

For years, she'd been praying that she would not succumb to temptation again. Then Nick drifted into town, which was bad enough. But here he was at church, tempting her to have wildly irrational thoughts about him staying in town and a future they might have together.

Utter nonsense. She knew better.

She gritted her teeth as the organ music crescendoed and the congregation rose for the first hymn.

Nick held out the hymnal, opened to the correct page, silently offering to share. She had no choice but to stand ever closer to him and grasp her side of the hymnal. Her shoulder brushed his, and she felt the heat of his body through his shirt and her cotton jacket. His baritone voice blended with her imperfect soprano, his words ringing with the power of welcoming God's bright morning sunlight.

Whew! *fans self* Lots of chemistry between these two. Ms. Carter also gives us a hint at the conflict with the line about *not succumbing to temptation again*. She doesn't want to make the same mistake with Nick that she made with another man in her past.

But the attraction is there all the same. We also get the heroine's physical or visceral reaction to being near the hero. We'll get more into that a little later, and how to show your characters' physical responses to being near each other.

Sexual tension is very much like other kinds of tension in a novel. You have to pull it slowly, let out a little slack here and there, then pull it tight again. It's an emotional manipulation that gives your reader a stake in the outcome of the book.

5. THE FIVE SENSES

Using the five senses grounds the reader in a scene and deepens the point of view, drawing them deeper into the story.

Let's face it. Sex is messy and sweaty and *physical*. That is if you're doing it right. *wink* This is where the five senses really come into play. You're not going to use all five in one scene, but be aware of which ones you're using, when, how, and why. What information are you giving the reader about your characters' mindset and how turned on they're getting?

Sight

From the first time your characters see each other naked to the millionth time, there will be visual impact. Men especially are very visual. What do your characters notice about each other? How does watching their partner slowly undress for them impact their desire? What new things do they notice about their partner's body and/or face? But don't get so bogged down in what your characters are seeing that you forget about the other four senses.

Scent

There are lots of smells bombarding your characters when they're up close and personal with a partner. How the heroine's hair smells. The way the hero's sweaty, glistening skin smells. Sex itself has a smell, as do certain areas of the body. There's also the undetectable scent of pheromones that stimulates our sex drive. What's important about the scents your character experiences?

Scent is one of the senses that we use to choose a potential mate whether we realize it or not. I once watched a TV show where they did an experiment with scent. They had ten men each wear a white t-shirt for a day. Then they bagged them and numbered them. They then had ten women smell each shirt and rate how attracted to the scent they were. As a test, one of the ten men was a blood relative to each of the women. The women unknowingly ranked the man they were related to very low. The experiment showed that scent plays an important role in selecting the most viable mate

—the mate with a genetic makeup that is dissimilar to their own, thus improving their chances of having healthy offspring.

Interesting, huh?

Touch

You can't have sex without touching. From a light caress to a tight grip, sex is a very physical activity in which most parts of the characters' bodies will come into contact and hands become *very* important. Where and how the characters touch each other will show the progression and level of trust in the relationship. The more intimate the touch, the closer the couple is to each other.

Taste

Unless your characters eat a meal, you're not likely to use the sense of taste very often in your novel. But sex scenes are where taste really shines. From the salty taste of sweat on skin to the taste of other bodily fluids, the mouth will be an active participant in sex scenes. It's difficult to write a sex scene without licking, sucking, and kissing. Lovers explore their partner's body with their hands *and* their mouth. What places on your character's body are particularly sensitive, and how can their partner heighten the sexual experience by exploring those erogenous zones?

Hearing

What sounds do your characters make during sex? Do they talk? What sounds fill the room? What sounds drift in from outside the intimate space the lovers are in? The slap of skin on skin, moaning, heavy breathing, throaty sounds, barked-out demands—sex is a noisy affair. Think about how you can use sound to turn up the heat on your love scenes.

6. SEX AND EMOTION

Sex engages our emotions. It's a game changer. A point of no return.

Romance is about a couple falling in love. It's one of the most powerful events in our life. Sex without emotion is erotica or porn. Since we're writing romance we need to engage the characters' emotions *and* the readers'. Sex has consequences emotionally. It can make you feel very close to a person very quickly. As I said before, the first sex scene will have a different feel and tone than the final sex scene in your novel. Feelings intensify the longer a couple is together and the more often they have sex. Use that budding emotional connection in your sex scenes.

The first sex scenes will be mostly physical, that scratching of the itch. The later sex scenes will be more emotional. To show this I often use different, softer language. The sex becomes less about physical sensation and more about how the characters feel about each other the further we get into the book. It shows how your characters begin to realize that they might not be able to live without one another and how hard they're willing to fight or how much they're willing to change to stay in the relationship.

Here's the first sex scene from **Lost** by Beth Yarnall:

"Touch me," she begged in the softest voice.

He dropped to his knees before her, giving her the advantage of height. He reached for her, bringing her against him. The feel of her skin on his nearly broke him, her kiss inflaming him to the point of madness. She threaded her fingers through his hair. He couldn't stop touching her, kissing her, licking her, pressing her to him. He wanted to be everywhere at once.

Her breasts, a miniature perfection, drew his immediate attention. With a hand on her ass, he clasped her to him. He traced a finger over the slight slope, down and around, closer each time, watching in fascination as her nipple pebbled for him just inches away. He'd never seen breasts so small and hadn't thought the size much mattered.

But hers... Jesus. He flicked his tongue out for a taste. She moaned and arched. So sensitive. He licked again, holding her as she leaned back, offering more. He took it. Her nipple in his mouth...

He could smell her. God he wanted her. Bare. All of her. Gripping the scrap of lace covering her, he yanked. The material ripped, gave way. She whimpered, her knees buckling as he slipped a finger in from behind. She was so hot, so wet, the scent of her... aw, damn. Had to have her. Had to taste her. *Now*.

He lifted her and threw back the covers, placing her close to the edge of the bed. She spread wide for him and he got his first look at her. So beautiful. His. She made a small noise as he knelt before her. One lick and she jerked, gripping the bed sheets. And then he set his mouth to her, loving her. She writhed and moaned, pressing her feet against his shoulders. He slipped in one finger, then another. Working her with his tongue and mouth he took his time, stimulating and soothing, he brought her to the edge.

"Oh, God," she begged. "Oh, my God. Oh, oh, ah..."

He sucked gently, swirling his tongue, pistoning his fingers and she came hard for him with a long low moan. He nearly lost it, holding onto her through her last shudders.

Had to be in her. *Now*. He stripped the rest of the way and reached into the bedside drawer. The condom secured, he returned to her. He nibbled her inner thigh and she twitched, reaching for him. He stretched out next to her, watching as he smoothed a hand up her thigh, over the flat of her stomach and back again.

She pulled him down for a kiss and he knew she could smell herself on him. Running her hands over him, she shifted and then he was there. Right there. Between her legs. He looked down. He had to go slow for her. Had to make it good. He held himself over her, careful to not crush her. She moved beneath him, tilting her hips in invitation.

It's mostly physical. This is the first time they have sex and they're finally scratching that itch. I cut the scene short of penetration, but I can assure you they go all the way. I feel like my point was made with this shortened example.

Let's revisit the lovers a little later in the book. Note the differences in the two scenes. A lot has happened between them from the first time they were together until now.

"I need this," she whispered in his ear. "I need you."

He shivered, a rippling of muscle. "You got me."

He scooped her up in one motion and carried her back through the living room and down the hall to the bedroom. He laid her down and went into the arms she stretched out to him. She wanted his weight on her, holding her down so she wouldn't fly apart. Needing the feel of skin on skin, she yanked at her clothing, then his. In seconds she got what she wanted, and that first moment when their flesh met settled something inside her, at the same time releasing a current of longing that sent her straight to him.

No one was like him. His hands, his mouth, his body did things for her that no one had ever done, would ever do. After the first flurry of movement to get naked, they slowed things down. His fingertips feathered over her skin, setting small fires in their wake. He savored her, she felt it in the way he looked at her and touched her. This would be no frenzied coupling. It would be slow and deliberate and before they were through they'd each have taken more and given more than they should have. She knew this and yet couldn't stop it, couldn't keep herself apart from him anymore.

She melted into the sensations, gave over to the

sweet ride and in return elicited long, drawn out sighs and sharp intakes of breath from him that only encouraged more. She pleasured him with her mouth and her hands, telling him with her body what words could never express. Holding nothing back, they gave until they shook with a need that might never be quenched.

And the moment he entered her she knew they'd crossed a threshold, could see it reflected back at her. He whispered words of endearment as he rocked into her, keeping pace with the hammering of her heart. Limbs entwined, bodies slick with sweat, hearts beating out a pounding rhythm, they found their release, a shattering climax that brought tears to her eyes. He shook with the after effects and she wrapped her limbs around him, anchoring him to her.

Their breathing slowed, but their hands kept moving, caressing, soothing. They'd been through a war, a rebirth. What they'd be on the other side, she didn't know. She should be scared, but all she could do was accept.

He tucked her tight against him as they drifted toward slumber. "*Mi amor*," he murmured in a voice almost too quiet to be heard. But she'd heard and understood. *My love.*

Ah, the L-word. This scene is about how far they've come and how far they're willing to go to be together. They're emotionally invested now. It's no longer about just scratching that itch, but about two people connecting in a very real way.

7. VISCERAL REACTIONS

As I said, sex is very physical. You burn calories getting busy. On average men burn 100 calories and women burn 69 (oh yes, you read that right). Sexual desire and emotional investment, as well as the exertion of the act, have a physical effect on the body. Hearts beat faster. Breath rates increase. Perspiration coats the skin. Limbs might shake. Not to mention the effect arousal has on genitals. There's a lot going on in the mind *and* the body.

Here's an excerpt from **Too Much Temptation** by Lori Foster (one of my all-time favorite books—the sex scenes are *amazing*):

"Come here, Grace."

She gave him a questioning look even as she scooted up.

"Right here," he said, and patted his lower

abdomen. "I want you to face away from me. That way I can play with you all I want."

She went very still, her expression worried and hesitant. "I don't know how much more of this I can take, Noah."

That was pretty up-front for a virgin. "Trust me, Gracie. You can take plenty." Noah reached for her. "And you will."

She whimpered in a mix of excitement and dread. But she didn't fight him when Noah arranged her to his satisfaction, her back to his chest, her soft legs draped wide over his muscular thighs, her hands at her sides, palms flat on the mattress. With his mouth touching the side of her throat Noah said, "Now don't move, Gracie."

She moaned in anticipation. Noah cupped both her breasts, pulling gently at her swollen, sensitive nipples. "Most women," he told her, speaking above her panting breasts, "can feel this even between their legs. Can you?"

She nodded shakily and whimpered again.

"Feel good?"

With a broken gasp, she murmured, "*Too good.*"

"No such thing, sweetheart." Noah kissed her throat, determined to make her first experience memorable. "Let's just spend some time doing this, okay? I love your breasts."

Her back arched and he warned, "Be still now."

"I...I can't, Noah!"

Yes, you can." He opened his mouth on her shoulder, then closed his teeth down carefully on a muscle—and tugged at her nipples, tweaking, rolling.

Grace's fingers knotted in the sheet and her groan was deep and ragged. Noah took his time, teasing her and teasing himself until they were both breathing roughly. His erection nestled between Grace's firm bottom cheeks, snug and warm. He wanted to enter her this way, he decided.

Hell, he wanted to enter her every way, in every position imaginable.

He heard her give a soft sob, shaking uncontrollable, hand he smoothed his hands down her body to her belly. "Open your legs wider, Grace."

She quickly obeyed.

"Mmmmm," Noah said, staring down the length of her sprawled body and touching her with just his fingertips. "Damn. You're really close, aren't you? Do you see how swollen your little clitoris is?"

She gasped as he thumbed her, her hips jerking hard.

"You keep moving, Grace," he playfully chastised. "Hold still."

"*I can't.*"

Noah pushed two fingers into her. He entered easily now because she was so wet, but still he file her flinch. "You sore, baby?"

"No. Yes. A little." She strained against him. "You're big."

"Especially for this little virginal opening, huh?" He held his breath, waiting for her to reply, his fingers buried deep inside her. She was stretched taut around him, clenching his fingers in quick spasms. Noah felt certain Grace was a virgin, but he wanted to hear her admit it.

He wanted to know that she was his.

Her head pressed back into his shoulder and her buttocks squired against his erection. "Yes."

Savage emotions surged inside him. He hooked his free arm under her breasts and gunned her tight. It took him a moment before he could speak, and the nhe whispered, "Dou you want to come now, Grace?"

In this passage, we're in Noah's point of view, but we get some of Grace's visceral reactions as well as his own. He's reading her body language, figuring out what she likes and doesn't like. Ms. Foster made us feel everything the characters were feeling as they were feeling it, and gave us their physical reactions to what was happening in the scene.

There's a reason I've read *Too Much Temptation* at least three or four times. Ms. Foster not only delivers the sexy, she also builds a really strong romance between two imminently likeable characters.

8. IT'S NOT YOU—IT'S YOUR CHARACTERS.

How your characters act and react will be different from how *you* act and react during sex. Remember, we're not writing an autobiography here. Your characters may even have better sex than you. It happens. They also might be more sexually explorative than you. Or not, depending on their background, what turns them on, their insecurities, and the level of trust between the partners. It's not you having sex on the page—it's your characters.

The manner and frequency of the sexual encounters your characters have will differ from book to book. No two couples are alike, so no two sex scenes will be alike. Some of the acts may be similar, but how they react and respond will be wildly different. I have read authors who have gotten bored with writing sex scenes or their personal situation has affected their ability to really get into the love scenes they write. It's a shame. If I ever get to that point I'd rather not write those scenes, even if I have to change genres to do it.

Readers pick up on author boredom. They know when you're phoning it in. So if you're going to write sex scenes, imagine yourself as your characters. What turns them on? What turns them off? What surprises are discovered?

One of my favorite bed play discoveries is in **Welcome to Temptation** by Jennifer Crusie. Sophie discovers that the threat of being caught in the act is a huge turn on for her. Here's an excerpt:

She started to laugh, only to stop when she heard people in the kitchen downstairs. "Shhh."

"Why?" Phin stopped moving. "It's just Wes and Amy."

"Yeah." Sophie looked over her shoulder at the door.

"Did you lock it?" Phin said in her ear, and he sounded amused.

"I forgot." She tried to pull away from him, but he rolled and trapped her again, sliding deeper inside her and making her gasp. "Stop it," she said breathlessly. "I'm not even sure it's closed all the way. Let me go lock ti and I'll come back."

"Bothers you, huh?" Phin started working his

way down her neck again and he pulsed indie her, and Sophie felt the heat spread low as her blood pounded.

"No," she lied.

"They could walk in anytime." He nibbled on her shoulder, and she twitched under him and felt her breath go. "Walk right in and find us naked." He slid his hand up to her sweat-dampened breast, and the heat rolled across her as she moved to his rhythm. "Find you naked. With me inside you. *Nothing* you could do about it."

She caught her breath and said, "*Stop* it," and he said, "Nope, I think we're getting somewhere."

She squirmed under him to get away, and their bodies slid together. He said, "oh, God, yes, do that," and she smacked him on the shoulder because he was so impossible, and arched into him at the same time because he was so hard moving inside her and he felt so good.

"Maybe I can get...somebody else...to open that door," he said in her ear, and she said, "No!" a lot louder than she meant because it was part moan. She heard Amy say, "Sophie?" downstairs, and she tensed. Phin laughed down at her, his face as damp as hers.

Beautifully moist, Sophie thought. *Be careful what you wish for.*

Amy called her name again, and Phin said, "Excellent." He rocked higher into her, and she bit her lip to keep from moaning and then moaned anyway. "Louder," he said, and she shook her head as the heat built and his rhythm began to make her mindless.

"Then it's up to me." He sounded breathless. "The guy always has to do everything."

He leaned over her to the bedside table, and she bit into his shoulder from the sheer pleasure of feeling him against her. Then he stopped, and she looked up to see him holding the alarm clock.

"I'll buy you a new one," he said, and threw it against the wall.

"What are you *doing?*" she screamed as it crashed and went off clanging. Amy called up, "Sohpie?" and Phin moved again, rocking harder, and she shuddered under him and gasped, "*Stop* it."

"This close? Not on your life." He was moving faster now, and she clutched at him and breathed hard as the pressure built. She said, "No...no...we're not...close," and he rolled across her again, making her jerk against him. He picked up the dolphin lamp, yanking the cord out with it, and she realized what he was doing and shrieked, "No!" just as he threw it against the wall.

It shattered and fell on top of the clanging alarm.

"Sophie?" Amy called, and starred up the stairs, and Phin said, "This is it," and moved high into her, grabbing her wrists and holding them over her head, sliding hot on top of her, rocking hard inside her, whispering in her ear that Amy'd catch them, any minute, any minute, any minute, now, now, *now*, and Sophie twisted under him, caught in the heat and the slide and the panic and the throb he was pounding into her, and then Amy said, "Sophie?" and pushed open the door, and Sophie cried, "Oh, *God*," and came so hard she almost passed out.

"Oh," Amy said, and shut the door.

Sophie heard Amy go down the stairs, with only a fraction of her attention. The rest was consumed with how good she felt everywhere as the aftershocks made her twitch, how much she needed her breath back, and how she was going to strangle Phin when he let go of her writs and she was done feeling incredible. And even as she had the thought, he shuddered on top of her and let go, collapsing with his face in her pillow.

"You *pervert*," she said minutes later, when she could talk.

"You came," he said, his voice muffled by the pillow.

"I don't *believe* you did that."

"I don't believe you're not grateful."

"Grateful?" Sophie struggled to sit up, and for once he let her slide out from under him, rolling to get rid of the condom as she moved away from him.

"*Look* at this." The alarm clock was smashed next to the baseboard, and the dolphin lamp was in a million pieces, and it was just a *mess*, but try as she might, she couldn't work up any real indignation. Total satisfaction did that, she supposed, just sort of made everything else irrelevant. Still, he'd been impossible, so she concentrated on the carnage while she used the sheet to blot the sweat from her happily throbbing body. "I mean, just look at it!"

Phin draped his arm across her shoulders and pulled her back down on the bed, his face still in the pillow. "Did you come?"

Sophie crossed her arms over her breasts and glared at the ceiling, ignoring the hot weight of his arm across her and all the cheering her body was doing. "Yes."

"Did you like it?" he said, his voice still muffled by the pillow.

She started to grin in spite of herself. "Yes."

This is one of my favorite sex scenes I've ever read. Ms. Crusie really gets into the head and heart of her characters. It's a fun, light scene. Not all love scenes have to be about crazy, swing-from-the-chandeliers sex. There are lots of different ways a character can discover their partner's turn ons.

Here's a scene from ***Urge*** by Beth Yarnall:

He bent his head and kissed her, gently, as though this alone was all he wanted. She shifted beneath him, accustoming herself to his weight and the way they fit together. Sliding his hands into her hair, he deepened the kiss. Her body became heavy, languid in the first flush of desire. She shifted again and he settled between her legs, right where she most wanted him. Groaning, he ground against her. She brought her knees up and slid her feet up his legs, locking him to her.

Rocking her pelvis, she brought him right to her entrance. All he had to do was push into her. He was right there. So close. He pulled back, moving away from her. She made a noise of disappointment and followed him, using her feet to bring him back to her.

"God, Erin… I can't… I'm—"

She reached for him between their bodies. He gripped both of her hands suddenly and pinned them above her head.

"Stop doing that. I can't take—" His words ended in an incomprehensible grumble as she once again pressed her pelvis up, bringing him against her once more.

She thought she'd die without the feel of him inside her. She wanted him now, hard and fast. No gentleness, nothing slow or deliberate. She wanted a mindless coupling, a crude fucking. There'd be time for finesse later when the need wasn't so sharp. As if hearing her thoughts, he held her hands in one hand and slipped one, then two fingers inside of her, testing.

"Do it," she commanded. "Do it now."

"Stop it or I won't last two seconds."

"I don't care."

"That's what you say now," he murmured in her ear, stroking her. "I want you screaming as I pound into you. Over and over." He quickened the pace as she writhed against his hand. "Harder and harder. I want you to yell my name when you come."

Her breath came in short pants. She was so close. He nipped her earlobe, then sucked on it. But she held back. She wanted him with her. He held her hands tight and whispered naughty things in her ear, all the things he'd do to her. She struggled against his hold. Even though she could, she didn't break it. Her resistance brought her body in constant contact with his. Her whole body was on fire, burning to join with his. He coaxed her on.

The filthy things he promised drove her mad as erotic images played one after the other behind her closed eyelids.

Her loud gasps filled the room, nearly drowning out his words as he drove her wild with his dirty mouth and skilled hand. On the threshold of orgasm, she sucked in a stunned breath as he suddenly replaced his hand with his cock, pushing hard into her. Gripping the sheets, she came long and loud, shouting his name. He rocked into her once, twice and then he too reached his climax, muffling his groan in her neck.

His breath puffed against her heated skin, scattering goose bumps. She'd wanted mindless. What she'd gotten was earth altering and embarrassing. She squeezed her eyes shut, reliving the way she'd wantonly begged him to screw her, then got increasingly hotter at the dirty, almost disgusting suggestions he'd whispered in her ear. Is that what he thought of her? Did he think she wanted him to do all of those things to her? Her cheeks heated as she remembered the particular scenario he'd been filling her head with when she came.

She tried to disentangle herself from him, but he was still inside her. At her movement he stirred, sliding deeper into her until he hit her most sensitive spot. He pulled out, then in again, still hard within her. She attempted once more to get out from under him, but he gathered her to him.

"We did it your way, Babe," he whispered. "Now we'll do it mine."

He stroked into her, nearly all the way out, then deep. His movements were languid and deliberate as though he were learning her from the inside out. Her body reacted, flushing hot. Pleasure rippled through her. She ran her hands over his sweat-slickened body, down his back, clutching his bottom as he seated himself deep. The play of muscles beneath her hand thrilled her so much she moved to grip both cheeks as he plunged into her once more.

Smoothing her hair back, Graham kissed her as he'd intended to from the start, taking his time. But the tension was already building, pushing at him to plunge hard and fast into her. Sweet Jesus, the sounds she made. She wasn't quiet in her pleasure. He was quickly learning which touches brought her to the edge. How his mouth could make her squirm and the surprisingly naughty side of her that had shocked them both. He liked it all. He'd barely made it into her before it was all over for him. He'd take his time this go around and wouldn't let her push him.

But even as he made the vow, she gripped his

ass, her nails sinking into his flesh. Her cries urged him on, yanking on the leash of his control. Everything she did, every sound, every movement was maddening. He could have her a thousand times and never experience all the ways in which she could drive him wild. He picked up the pace, sweating with the effort to last longer this time. Bending his head, he sucked her nipple. She rocked into him, meeting his thrusts. But she held back.

He hit into her harder, faster. Her screams filled the room and yet she held out. He hooked an arm through her leg, then the other, pushing her into the bed. He'd meant to go slow, but she'd challenged him. Her pleasure was a goal he chased now with a single-minded determination that blotted everything else out, including his own impending orgasm. He fused his mouth to hers, muting her cries. Their panting and the hard slap of flesh on flesh filled the silence.

And then she broke, her back arching. He stiffened, his own release crashing into him. Releasing her legs, he collapsed down next to her. His mind blank, his heart pounding, he sucked in air. The room came into focus inches at a time, beginning with Erin's face, which was turned away from him. The long line of her neck beckoned for a kiss if he could only move. His gaze drifted down to her breasts, rising and falling as she too regained her breath. He'd had fantasies about those breasts. None of which he'd gotten to fulfill. Damn it.

"You have control issues," he said. Or at least that's what he'd intended to say. Only it came out more like *Thew haff conthrol isthues* as he still couldn't quite feel his tongue.

She turned toward him. "Is this more of your crappy seduction technique? Actually, I guess it would be your post seduction technique."

"My technique is not crappy. It got you off. Twice."

"Hmm... Well," she hedged.

"I never would have pegged you for a screamer." He grinned at her, stupidly pleased with her and, not to brag, himself as well. "A dirty girl, too."

"Shut up."

He chuckled and followed her as she tried to move out of his reach. With his lower body still pinning her to the mattress, she didn't get far.

"I liked that too," he said, nuzzling her neck.

"You're a degenerate."

"Hmm, maybe. I had to really stretch to come up with some of that stuff though."

"Not that far."

"No, not that far. I'm going to do some of that

stuff to you, you know," he said, circling her nipple with the tip of one finger.

She swatted his hand away. "I'm not interested."

But she broke out in goose bumps, her nipples tightening, giving away just how interested in some of that stuff she really was. His dick twitched at her reaction. With more encouragement like that and some time, she'd have him hard and ready for yet another round. He grinned at her.

"You're very pleased with yourself."

He shifted to lie next to her, yawning. "No, just you."

Erin discovers she *likes* dirty talk. Or else she only likes it with Graham. These are the kinds of discoveries that will keep your sex scenes fresh and new from book to book. Individualize your scenes for your characters. Have fun with them.

9. WRITING THE SEX SCENE

You're not writing a how-to manual here.

If you're writing for adults, your readers will already know how sex works. We've all had The Talk. We know about the birds and bees. Watch that your sex scenes don't read like your characters are putting together IKEA furniture, where tab A goes into slot B or C, or even D. Think of sex scenes as action scenes. Lots of stuff is happening. There will be thought. There will be emotion. There will be sensation. There may even be talking or yelling. There will be movement. And it will all be happening at the same time.

I'm going to say something that may surprise you—sex scenes are not about the physical act of sex. I know. Shocking, right? They're action scenes that move the romance plot forward. They're a conversation or an exchange of information between bedmates. Your characters will learn a lot about each other and themselves in bed.

One of the ways I can tell a sex scene is working is if I get so caught up in writing it that I have a visceral reaction. Yep. It happens. When I was writing my novels **Lost** and **Saved**, I got physically warm. Those two were so *hot* for each other that *they* affected *me*. I think that's an important distinction to make and one that often gets confused. Thus the questions I get—and you might get—about my books reflecting my personal life.

I'm sure you've written a scene that made you smile or one that made you cry. It's the same with sex scenes. If there's no reaction in the writer there won't be a reaction in the reader. Not to say that the goal is to tantalize your readers, but if your characters' physical interactions aren't real enough or deep enough to affect you, your reader is going to have a difficult time believing your lovers as a couple. Your sex scenes will feel flat or disconnected. You must achieve deep point of view in every scene, *especially* sex scenes. You want your reader to be in the head and heart of your characters.

Deep point of view is so important in writing

that I wrote a book about it called ***Going Deep Into Deep Point of View***. Check it out or take a workshop or class if you don't understand deep point of view. It's essential to making sure your novel doesn't leave a dent in your reader's wall.

10. SEX AFTER RAPE OR SEXUAL ASSAULT

As I said earlier, romance novels deliver hope. Hope that a reader can have a happily ever after just like the characters in their favorite book. And no one deserves that HEA more than a survivor of rape or sexual assault. If you've never experienced sexual assault or rape you might want to do some research, read some blogs or talk with a survivor you know. Be sensitive of stereotypes.

How your character handles sex after an assault will be unique to them as an individual. How their partner reacts will be important too. It may take them a while to absorb and figure out how to work past it with their loved one.

In my novel **Fake**, Lucy, the heroine, is a rape and domestic abuse survivor. I not only had to put myself in her shoes, but also the shoes of Cal, the man who loves her. I thought long and hard about how he would react and how he would try to help Lucy. It wasn't easy. There were some difficult scenes between them, with a lot of conflicting emotions. It was tough. I cried a lot for them, then smiled through the tears when they found their happily ever after.

11. SEX IN THE AGE OF HIV

Sex in the Age of HIV

To wrap or not to wrap?

Sex has consequences. Certainly there's a risk of pregnancy, but there's also the risk of sexually transmitted diseases. Romance authors will often have their characters use condoms. There will most likely be some kind of conversation between the characters about birth control, maybe even about being 'clean'—i.e. testing negative for HIV.

Then again, there might be no mention of birth control whatsoever. These days anything goes. Again, we're writing for adults. We don't need to explain the risks or options to our readers. We're also creating a bit of a fantasy. The reader will assume that your hero and heroine are disease free unless you tell them otherwise. I have yet to read a romance where a character is HIV positive. That doesn't mean they're not out there. In fact, I'd really like to read one to find out how the author tackled the situation.

Readers should be able to find a romance novel in which they see themselves, no matter their chosen gender, race, religion, experience, sexual preference or HIV status. One of the great things about reading and writing romance is the hope it brings. Everyone deserves love. We all need it. It's exciting when we find a book that reflects our lives or the life we wish we had.

In real life—condoms, condoms, condoms. In fiction we can bend reality a bit for effect. But if you want to incorporate the use of condoms in your novel, make it fun. Here's a scene from my novel, **Saved**, in which I play with the putting on of a condom.

He returned a moment later and reached past her to turn the stove off.

"What are you doing? I wasn't done cooking."

In answer he wrapped his arms around her from behind, pressing his erection against her.

"Are you serious? I have to leave for work in less than an hour and I haven't even showered yet." He nibbled her neck, his hands roaming north and south. She made that little sighing squeak sound he loved. "All right, but make it quick. And good. It better be good."

He found her already wet for him and moaned at the feel of her heat. He moved her away from the stove and lifted her onto the counter, wedging between her legs as he'd imagined. He slapped a condom down on the counter next to her and kissed her long and deep until she was squirming against him.

"You're a naughty boy," she panted, giving him a playful whack on the backside with the spatula.

He grabbed a fistful of her shirt in back and pulled it tight across her chest. Dipping his head, he captured her nipple in his mouth, sucking through the thin cotton. She gasped, and reached for the fastening of his pants as the spatula clattered to the floor. She managed to get both hands on him, stroking him. She spread a bead of moisture across the tip with her thumb. He patted the counter blindly, searching for the condom, his mouth now at her other breast.

"Looking for this?"

He broke away to find her twirling the condom between two fingers. He reached for it.

"Nuh-uh. I'll do it." She bit the edge of the foil and tore slowly, a naughty glint in her eye.

Damn, she was hot.

Using her feet she pushed his pants down where they pooled at his ankles. She scooted to the edge of the counter. "Now hold real still. I want to make sure I get this on just right."

He widened his stance, gripping her thighs for balance. She made a show of getting the condom on right side up, faking a couple of false starts. He shifted his feet, watching her every move. She turned it one way, then the other swirling it over the crown, teasing him. She used both hands to roll it all the way down, slow as if she had all the time in the world. Wrapping both hands around him, she smoothed up then down, up, then down...

"It's on," he bit out.

"Just making sure." She blinked up at him all wide innocent eyes.

Two could play at that game.

Condoms *can* be fun!

12. GETTING IN THE MOOD

Getting in the Mood

How do you write a sex scene when you're not feeling particularly sexy?

Create a mood for yourself. Light a candle. Dim the lights. Pour yourself a glass of wine. Listen to some sexy music. Watch a sexy scene on TV. Whatever works for you. I have a playlist just for sex scenes. Songs that inspire.

When you're working toward a deadline you don't always have the luxury of writing 'insert sex scene here' and a brief description of the tone of the scene, then moving on. Start as you mean to go, I always say.

I actually find it more difficult to insert a placeholder, then come back and write the scene later, than to just write the scene as it comes. I like to be in the headspace of the characters and fresh on the events leading up to the sex scene when I write it. If the characters are working up towards sex it's a lot easier for me to just keep writing straight on through. But do what works for you. Like I said, there is no *right way* to write a book.

13. RESEARCH

Again, we're not writing autobiographies.

The best way to write romance and sex scenes is to read them. Find the level of sexual involvement you're comfortable with, whether that's sweet, sexy or erotic, and read it extensively. Not only will you learn genre norms, but you'll also learn reader expectations—the do's and don'ts.

I've also found YouTube to be a valuable tool. There are videos for *everything*, including sex. Don't know how to perform oral sex on a woman? Watch an instructional video. Don't know how anal sex could possibly work? Watch a video. One of my favorites demonstrates on fruit, but I've also found some that use real-looking, waist-down dummy torsos. If you're squeamish about watching a video there are tons of books and how-to manuals online.

The Kama Sutra has been a classic for decades for a reason.

There are also a lot of instructional websites. The Internet is a vast and marvelous place, but tread lightly. You don't want to accidentally discover something illegal or disturbing. But please do your due diligence. There's nothing like the mental record-scratching sound when a reader halts mid sex scene to wonder if the author understands how sex works. Embarrassing. Don't be the writer who uses spit as lubricant in an anal sex scene. It's not the same as lube. Trust me on this.

14. IN CLOSING...

Sadly all great things must come to an end. I hope you've learned something new about writing romance and sex scenes (and maybe even sex itself!). At least enough to attempt writing a love scene, even if it doesn't end up in your finished novel. Actually, write more than one. The more you write the better you'll become. Writing sex scenes is like riding a bicycle...or having sex. The more you do it, the more expert you'll be. Stretch your skills. Expand your writerly repertoire.

And by all means, (say it with me now) DON'T BE ORDINARY.

*****

If you enjoyed the excerpts from my novels you can find my full list at:
➤https://www.bethyarnall.com/CronologicalBooklist

Join my VIP Facebook group Babes with Books for exclusive sneak peeks at my upcoming books:
➤www.facebook.com/groups/BabesWithBooksReaderGroup

Sign up to receive my newsletter for new release alerts, exclusive bonus content, and giveaways!
➤www.bethyarnall.com/newsletter

ALSO BY BETH YARNALL

DANGEROUS LINES

Lost

Saved

Fake

Real

Urge

Rare

Betray

RECOVERED INNOCENCE

Liberate

Exonerate

Vindicate

INNOCENT SERIAL

Episode One

Episode Two

Episode Three

THE MISADVENTURES OF MAGGIE MAE

Wake Up, Maggie

You're Mine, Maggie

Find Me, Maggie

AZALEA MARCH MYSTERIES

Dyed and Gone

BETH WRITING AS BETTY PAPER

CRAZY ON YOU

Captive

Tinsel

Piano Lessons

BETH'S BOOKS FOR WRITERS

Crafting Unputdownable Fiction series

Going Deep Into Deep Point of View

Making Description Work Hard For You

Some Like It Hot: Writing Sex and Romance

ABOUT THE AUTHOR

USA Today best selling author and Rita® finalist, Beth Yarnall, writes mysteries, romantic suspense, and the occasional hilarious tweet. She lives in Southern California with her husband, two sons, and their rescue dogs where she is hard at work on her next novel. For more information about Beth and her novels please visit her website-www.bethyarnall.com

- facebook.com/bethyarnallauthor
- amazon.com/author/bethyarnall
- bookbub.com/authors/beth-yarnall

BIBLIOGRAPHY

Lost by Beth Yarnall
   Copyright © 2012 Elizabeth Yarnall

Saved by Beth Yarnall
   Copyright © 2012 Elizabeth Yarnall

Fake
   Copyright © 2014 Elizabeth Yarnall

Real by Beth Yarnall
   Copyright © 2014 Elizabeth Yarnall

Urge
   Copyright © 2015 Elizabeth Yarnall

Rare by Beth Yarnall

Copyright © 2015 Elizabeth Yarnall

Innocence serial by Beth Yarnall
　　Copyright © 2015 Elizabeth Yarnall

Liberate by Beth Yarnall
　　Copyright © 2016 Elizabeth Yarnall

Far From Honest by Beth Yarnall
　　Copyright © 2017 Elizabeth Yarnall

Home to Montana by Charlotte Carter
　　Copyright © 2013 Charlotte Lobb
　　Harlequin Enterprises Limited Ontario, Canada

Too Much Temptation by Lori Foster
　　Copyright © 2002 Lori Foster
　　Zebra Books, an imprint of Kensington Publishing Corp New York, New York

Welcome to Temptation by Jennifer Cruise
　　Copyright © 2000 Jennifer Cruise Smith
　　St. Martin's Press New York, New York

Going Deep Into Deep Point of View by Beth Yarnall
　　Copyright © 2016 Elizabeth Yarnall

Intimate Behaviour by Desmond Morris
    Copyright © 1971 Desmond Morris
    Published by Vintage Digital, an imprint of Random House, a division of Penguin Random House LLC, New York

GMC: Goal, Motivation, and Conflict
    Copyright © 1996 Debra Dixon
    Published by Gryphon Books for Writers
    Memphis, Tennessee

Made in United States
Orlando, FL
29 July 2024